Pa Lia's First Day

MICHELLE EDWARDS

Harcourt Brace & Company

San Diego   New York   London

Requests for permission to make copies of any part of the work should
be mailed to: Permissions Department, Harcourt Brace & Company,
6277 Sea Harbor Drive, Orlando, Florida 32887-6777.

Library of Congress Cataloging-in-Publication Data
Edwards, Michelle.
Pa Lia's first day/Michelle Edwards.
p. cm.—(A Jackson friends book.)
Summary: On the first day of second grade at her new school,
Pa Lia Vang discovers that things are not as bad as she had feared.
ISBN 0-15-201974-X
[1. Schools—Fiction. 2. Friendship—Fiction.] I. Title. II. Series.
PZ7.E262Pal 1999
[Fic]—dc21   98-28567

First edition
A C E F D B
Printed in Hong Kong

The illustrations in this book were done in pen and ink, ink wash,
and white paint on Arches Hot Press watercolor paper.
The display type was set in Worcester Round Medium.
The text type was set in Sabon.
Jacket and case color separations by Bright Arts Ltd., Hong Kong
Printed by South China Printing Company, Ltd., Hong Kong
This book was printed on Arctic matte paper.
Production supervision by Stanley Redfern
Designed by Lydia D'moch and Michelle Edwards

In appreciation and admiration,
to Mrs. Dykstra, Mrs. Foster,
Mrs. Johnson, Mrs. Keyes,
and Mrs. Sanford . . .
best in Frogtown and in my heart

And to Carol Dye, a dream librarian

Contents

Pa Lia

Pa Lia Vang skipped over the cracks in the sidewalk. She watched ants march between blades of grass. She tried to call a cat down from a tree.

1

"Pa Lia, quit your dawdling," said her brother, Tou Ger. She stopped to tie her shoes.

"Pa Lia, hurry up!" shouted Tou Ger.

But Pa Lia did not want to hurry. It was the first day of school and she was going to be a new kid at Jackson Magnet.

Pa Lia's legs felt heavy and stiff when she thought about being in a big new school filled with

strangers. Her mouth felt like it was
stuffed with cotton when
she thought about
meeting her teacher,
Mrs. Fennessey.
Her stomach felt like
it was filled with

a thousand fluttering butterflies when
she thought about walking alone into
her classroom.

Would everyone stare at her?

3

Tou Ger had promised to take Pa Lia right to the classroom door. He was older and bigger and braver. And he wasn't shy at all.

Pa Lia stopped to wipe her glasses. On the other side of the street, she could see a big red brick building—Jackson Magnet. She walked closer to Tou Ger.

"Cross," he told her. Pa Lia took his hand.

"Finally, we're here," announced Tou Ger.

Pa Lia stopped to tie her shoes

again. Slowly, she made two bunny
ears.

"Pa Lia, you are going to make me
late," warned Tou Ger. "If you don't
get up right this minute, I'm going into
school without you."

Pa Lia closed her eyes. She tugged
at her long black braids. She wished
a hundred hungry tigers would all roar
at Tou Ger. She wished he
would stop telling her to
hurry up. *He isn't the
boss of me*, Pa Lia
thought.

She opened her eyes. Tou Ger was
gone!

Pa Lia searched around her. *How could he leave me all alone on the first day of school?*

Pa Lia chewed on a braid. She bit her nails. *How will I find my classroom by myself?*

Pa Lia looked at all the kids on the playground. Kids walking, kids getting off buses, and kids getting out of cars. Kids who knew where they were going.

Pa Lia felt like a teeny-tiny minnow in a huge giant ocean.

All Alone

Jackson Magnet was a great big school. Pa Lia's classroom was somewhere up the steep stone steps and through the wide wooden doors.

Pa Lia studied the steps. She saw a group of little kids walking carefully. They giggled and whispered.

Kindergartners, she thought.

She watched four boys with big backpacks. They jumped up the steps, two at a time.

Pa Lia spied three older girls. They were chewing gum and talking loud and fast. They looked like they had been going to Jackson Magnet for a million years.

Pa Lia followed them up the steps. She squeezed through the doors with them. The older girls raced up the stairs. Pa Lia took a deep breath.

Jackson Magnet smelled just like the first day of school. Pa Lia could smell new shoes, new pencils, and clean floors. She could hear the loud buzz of kids talking and yelling. Jackson was a noisy place.

Pa Lia slowly climbed a few stairs. She looked down at the first floor. She looked up at the second floor. She stood still to think a minute.

At her old school, the kindergarten, first grade, and second grade were all on one floor. Would the second grade at Jackson be on the first floor or the second floor? Pa Lia wished she knew.

"Hey, four-eyes!" someone yelled. "Move it!"

Pa Lia turned around quickly and fell down two steps. Her backpack slid off one shoulder. Her knee and elbow ached.

Pa Lia wanted to cry.

Calliope

"Matthew Stern, cut it out, you dumb old stinker!" shouted a tall blond girl. She held out her hand to help Pa Lia up. "Hi. My name is Calliope James," she said.

Pa Lia took Calliope's hand. She stood up. "I'm Pa Lia Vang," she said softly.

"You must be new. I've never seen you before. Who's your teacher?" asked Calliope.

"Mrs. Fennessey."

"Then we're in the same class," said

Calliope. "And so is Matthew. We call him Stinky Stern, the enemy of the second grade."

Pa Lia sucked on her braid. Stinky Stern, a kid who called other kids mean names—a kid who

was the enemy of the second grade—
was going to be in her class.

"My best friend,
Howie, has Mrs.
Fennessey, too,"
said Calliope. "I
think you'll like
her. Howie's really
nice." Calliope smiled. She had a dimple in one cheek and a space between
her two front teeth. "Want to walk to
class together?"

"OK," said Pa Lia.

They walked up the rest of the stairs
and down a long, wide hallway. They
stopped in front of room 201.

"Here's our room," said Calliope.

Pa Lia read the WELCOME sign over

the door. She had made it to her class-room without Tou Ger.

"I'll bet Howie is already here." said Calliope. "Her bus is always early."

Pa Lia straightened her glasses. Her hands were sweaty. She wiped them on her shirt. *Now I'm going to meet Howie.*

Pa Lia sighed.

201

Mrs. Fennessey

Howie

Pa Lia peeked into room 201. She saw Mrs. Fennessey, a lot of kids, and a big room. Pa Lia was glad that Calliope was with her.

"Howie's here," said Calliope. She grabbed Pa Lia's hand. They walked toward a chubby girl with two pigtails and warm brown eyes.

"Pa Lia, meet my best friend, Howardina Geraldina Paulina Maxina Gardenia Smith—Howie for short. Howie, meet my new friend, Pa Lia Vang."

"Hi, Howie," said Pa Lia.

Howie looked just like a soft, cuddly teddy bear. Pa Lia wanted Howie to like her.

22

She smiled her biggest smile.

Howie did not smile back.

"I'm Howardina Geraldina Paulina Maxina Gardenia Smith to you," said Howie, and she walked away.

Pa Lia pushed her bangs out of her eyes. *Howie does not want to be my friend,* she thought.

"Howie!" called Calliope, and she walked over to Howie.

Pa Lia watched Howie and Calliope.

Calliope took a little stuffed monkey from her backpack and showed

it to Howie. Howie hugged the little monkey. She laughed and gave it back to Calliope. Calliope laughed and hugged the little monkey.

Pa Lia wished she could hug the little monkey, too. *Why did Howie and Calliope walk away from me?*

Room 201 was noisy. All the kids were busy talking—all except Pa Lia. *I'm all alone again,* she thought.

Cookies

"Quiet down!" said Mrs. Fennessey.

The first day of school was about to begin.

"Welcome, young people, to second grade," Mrs. Fennessey told the class. "Second grade is not kindergarten and it is not first grade. There is a lot to learn. We work very hard in second grade."

Next Mrs. Fennessey assigned seats. Howie and Calliope and Pa Lia were all in the row by the windows. Pa Lia would sit up front. Calliope was next. Then Howie.

Pa Lia went to her desk quickly and quietly.

Mrs. Fennessey didn't fool around. "Math will be first thing every day, starting today," she said. Then she explained what they would do in second-grade math.

$6 + 2 =$

$10 + 2 = 8$

$2 = 12$

$4 + 2 = 6$

$8 + 8 = 16$

$12 + 10 = 22$

$20 + 8 = 28$

$8 + 12 = 31$

$25 + 12$

While Pa Lia listened, she drew butterflies all over her new notebook.

She was about to start a flower when she heard Howie and Calliope whispering. Pa Lia turned around. *Are they whispering about me?* she wondered.

Pa Lia saw Howie pass two cookies to Calliope. Howie gave Pa Lia a dirty look.

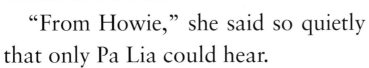

Calliope passed a cookie to Pa Lia.

"From Howie," she said so quietly that only Pa Lia could hear.

A cookie from Howie? Pa Lia didn't

 think so. She tasted the cookie. It was yummy. Maybe there was a way she could get Howie to like her. *Maybe me and Howie and Calliope can be friends.* Pa Lia had an idea.

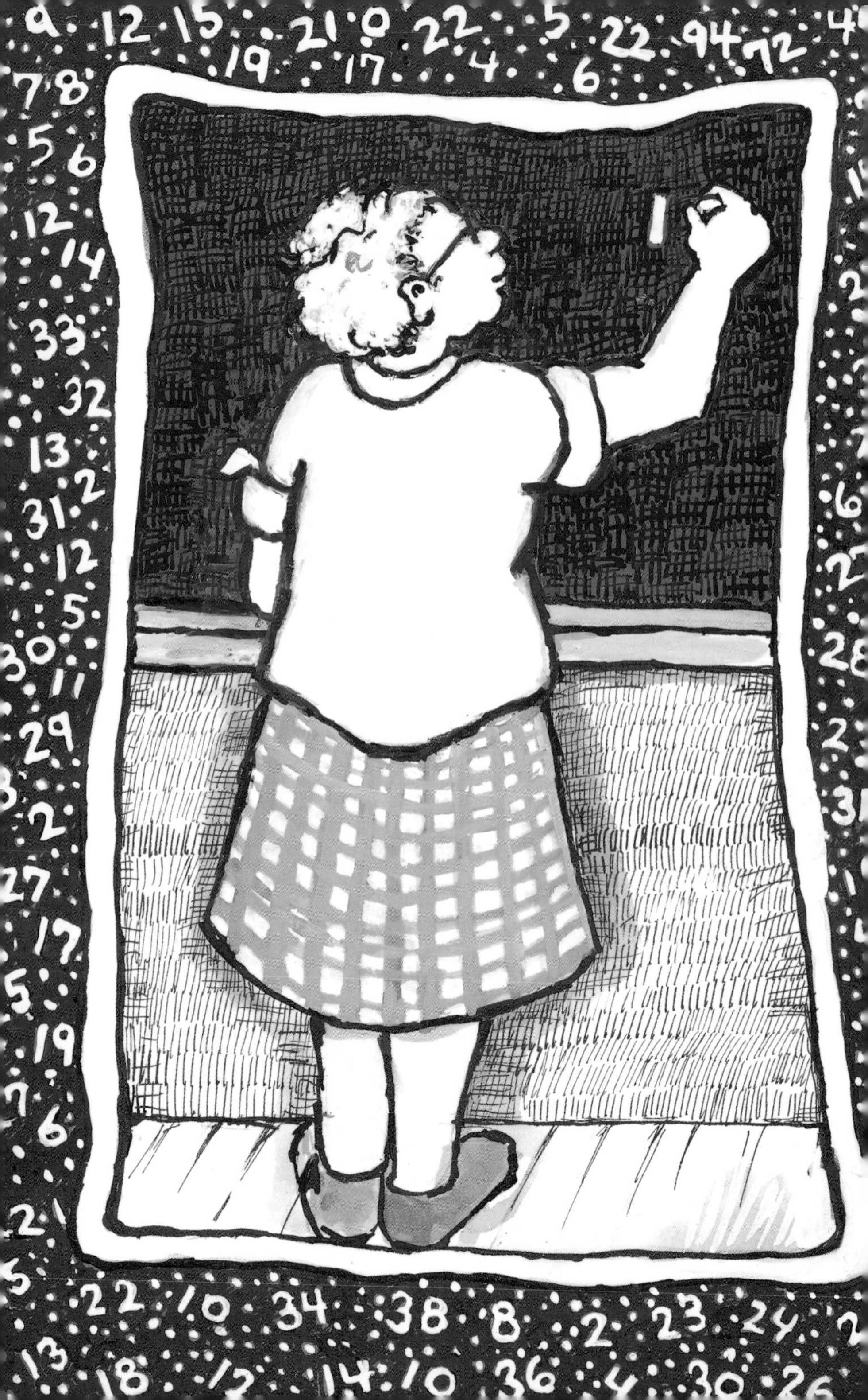

The Idea

"Now let's see what you remember from first grade," said Mrs. Fennessey. She filled the blackboard with subtraction problems. "Please write your name at the top of a clean sheet of paper. Then copy these problems and solve them."

Mrs. Fennessey sat down at her desk. She looked very busy.

Pa Lia took a sheet of paper from her notebook. She drew a picture of a mouse with freckles eating a cookie. The mouse was saying, "Crunch, crunch, crunch." She folded the paper in half and wrote *Calliope* on it.

Pa Lia took another sheet of paper. She drew a little mouse with pigtails eating a cookie. The mouse was saying, "Yummy, yummy, yummy. Thank you from my tummy." Pa Lia folded that paper in half, too. She wrote *Howard-ina* on it.

Pa Lia turned and quietly passed the notes to Calliope.

Calliope turned and passed one note on to Howie.

Pa Lia heard paper rustle. She heard a big laugh. It was Howie.

"Howardina, is something funny?" asked Mrs. Fennessey. "Would you like to share it with us?"

"She must have looked in the mirror," said Stinky Stern.

Pa Lia heard paper rustle again. She heard a medium-size laugh. Mrs. Fennessey heard it, too.

"Calliope, perhaps you can tell us what is so funny," said Mrs. Fennessey.

Room 201 was silent.

Thump, thump, thump. Pa Lia could hear her heart beating.

Mrs. Fennessey was mad at Howie and Calliope because they had laughed.

Thump, thump, thump. Howie and Calliope had given her a cookie and she had got them into trouble. *What should I do?* wondered Pa Lia.

Mrs. Fennessey asked again, "Could someone please tell me what is so funny?"

No one answered.

Mrs. Fennessey is waiting for an answer.

No Notes

Pa Lia's stomach hurt. *Mrs. Fennessey is waiting for an answer,* she thought.

If Pa Lia told her about the notes, she would get in trouble, too. Pa Lia never got into any trouble at her old school. *Will Mrs. Fennessey call my mother?*

Mrs. Fennessey walked over to Pa Lia's row. She was tall, like a gigantic oak tree.

"Howardina and Calliope, please stand up. Are you young ladies ready to tell me what is so funny?" asked Mrs. Fennessey.

"Mrs. Fennessey," said Pa Lia in a voice so tiny that no one could hear her. *I have to tell Mrs. Fennessey that I made Howie and Calliope laugh. It was not their fault.*

"Mrs. Fennessey," said Pa Lia in a bigger voice. She felt as if a huge wave were pushing her to speak louder. She felt like the wind about to howl.

"Yes, Pa Lia. What is it?" asked Mrs. Fennessey.

"I passed notes to Howardina and Calliope," Pa Lia said in a loud, shaky voice. She stood up. "I drew funny pictures. My pictures made them laugh."

Mrs. Fennessey looked Pa Lia in the eye. "In second grade at Jackson Magnet, we do not pass notes," she said. "Do you girls understand that?"

"Yes, Mrs. Fennessey. I'm sorry," said Pa Lia.

Mrs. Fennessey looked at Calliope.

 "Yes, Mrs. Fennessey. I'm sorry," said Calliope.

Mrs. Fennessey looked at Howie.

"Yes, Mrs. Fennessey. I'm sorry," said Howie.

"You may all sit down now," said Mrs. Fennessey.

Pa Lia, Calliope, and Howie sat down.

Pa Lia's face turned hot and red.

Calliope coughed.

Howie's chair squeaked.

Stinky Stern farted.

The bell rang for recess.

Friends

Pa Lia raced out of the room. She wanted to hide. She had made Mrs. Fennessey mad. She had got Calliope and Howie into trouble. They would never be her friends now.

I will never have any friends at Jackson, Pa Lia thought. Everyone would think she was a stinker, just like Matthew Stern. Passing notes and getting other kids in trouble on the

first day of school was a stinker thing to do. No one would want to be friends with a kid like that.

Pa Lia ran down the stairs as fast as she could. She was scared of Howie. She was scared of Calliope. *What will they say about me?*

Pa Lia heard footsteps. She  felt a warm hand grab her left hand and a cool one grab her right hand.

"You are something else, Pa Lia Vang," said Howie. "Something *brave*. It was brave how you stood up and told the truth."

"Howie's right," said Calliope. "And your drawings are *really* funny."

Pa Lia grinned. Howie and Calliope were not mad at her. They thought she was brave. They thought her drawings were funny. Howie and Calliope liked her!

"Thanks for the cookie, Howardina," said Pa Lia.

"You can call me Howie." She gave Pa Lia a big, warm teddy bear smile. "I'll bring some more tomorrow."

"Yummy, yummy, yummy. Thank

you from my tummy," Pa Lia and Howie sang together.

"I like that song," said Calliope. "What kind of cookies are you going to bring tomorrow?"

"Snickerdoodles," said Howie.

Calliope and
Howie kept right
on walking and
talking.
    Pa Lia
stopped and
looked up
at Jackson
Magnet. She
thought about
the morning.
Tou Ger had

left her all alone, and she had found
Calliope. She had passed notes during
math, and she had got into trouble. She
had told Mrs. Fennessey the truth,
and now Howie and Calliope thought
she was brave. She felt brave.

Pa Lia stared at the big red brick building. The halls were wide and the kids were noisy, but it was not scary anymore.

"Hey, Howie! Hey, Calliope!" Pa Lia shouted. "Wait for me!"